THE JOURNEY

The Quest for Meaning

"A Modern American Fable"

THE SPIRIT WALKERS

The Yeti, Sasquatch-Big Foot

An Excerpt from <u>The Journey</u>; Pages 161-208

<u>www.amazon.com/dp/0991502914</u>

ISBN: 978-0-9915029-3-6

The Spirit Walkers
Table of Contents

The Yeti, Sasquatch-Big Foot

The Cascades

The Path of the Spirit Walkers

The Marriage of Rahoo and Hoora

The Teachings of Nature

Purity of Being

The Little Ones

The Invisible

The Humans

The Great Darkness

Out of Africa / The Spirit Walkers

The Struggle

The Great Escape

The Ice Bridge

The Wall

David and Golith

Free At Last

An Unforgivable Future

The Illusion

Unidentified Flying Objects

Farewell.......

Preview:

The Journey / The Quest for Meaning

In the Shadows of the Dead / Vietnam 1968/69

The Yeti, Sasquatch-Big Foot

Join Marcus on this epic journey through time and space as he travels across America to discover Nature's basic truths. This is just one of many adventures in his life's story; **The Journey**. This is a metaphysical journey that starts and ends where it all begins. This is a journey through a Universe of circles that sets all things into motion and fills our lives with awe and wonder; *Birth-Death, With Life In Between*.

Born in the Allegany Mountains, Marcus wants to know the answers to his many questions. Why does it rain? Why does the sun come up every day to chase the night away? Why does he exist? He has to leave the protection of his family (the sacred circle) to answer these questions and discover the meaning of life. He must risk it all to journey forward. Bravely he steps off into the great unknown.

Marcus heads west. He travels through a vast forest, down its mighty rivers into the Great Plains and across the deserts. On his journey Marcus meets many of Nature's wild creatures: Eclipse the raven, Jetta the black widow, Badger the outlaw, Justice the white buffalo, Walking Moon the warrior chief, Midnight the bat, the scorpion, Coyote, Seal, Geo, the voices from the forest, Mother Condor, mother and brother bear, the Keeper, Chaos, and many others. His encounters with these beings teach him much. There are those who will do him harm and those who will protect him with their lives.

Marcus, a young raccoon, learns many lessons on his journey and commits himself to follow Nature's narrow path. This path leads him into the Cascade Mountains where an invisible force of Nature confronts Marcus and his best friend Coyote. Marcus and Coyote are challenged by the Spirit Walkers who are the guardians of the forest. The Spirit Walkers are dedicated to protect the forest and all the wild things that depend on it to survive. Join Marcus and Coyote on this narrow trail and discover who the Yeti really are and why they protect the forest from the humans.

The Spirit Walkers

The Cascades

Marcus had been on a long journey since he left the Allegany Mountains and his parents' home years before. After several misadventures and some poor choices he was befriended by his constant companion Coyote. Together they had traveled across the Sonoran Desert into Mexico and up the coast of California. They became the dear friends of a fun loving wave runner named Seal and got caught up in the hip scenes of their times. They were moving and grooving with all the happenings on the west coast until Seal's luck ran out; eaten by a whale on the last wave of his young life.

Broken hearted Marcus and Coyote made their way back up into the highlands and began their long trek into the Sierra Nevada Mountains. They moved down from the Sierras up into the Cascades. After traveling over a thousand miles together they finally reached the southern fringes of the Cascade Mountains. The mountain range in which Geo had promised they would find the fire-mountains.

As they traveled up into the mountains the forest became dense and rich with foliage. A bounty of ferns and thick patches of moss were everywhere. The moss was several inches deep completely covering the forest floor.

Only the animal trails occasionally revealed the soil hidden beneath this precious carpet of green. It was as if an invisible gardener created this mystical landscape and weaved this one path through the middle of her masterpiece leaving the rest of her delicate creation untouched, pristine and flawless.

The trees towered above Coyote and Marcus with the branches and leaves melting into an emerald canopy that in many places blotted out the sun. During the early hours of the day moisture blanketed every plant below the canopy. Without a cloud in the sky, water drips from the leaves and branches of the trees creating a rain forest that never completely dries. One would have to climb to the upper branches to find the sun and unbroken light. Only there would you be able to escape the wetness of this forest.

·················

Coyote and I had been on this narrow trail for two days and it was approaching dark when we heard a strange and terrifying howl in the distance. This was not quite a howl, nor one of the typical animal calls we were familiar with. It was bone piercing; like nothing we had ever heard before.

It was oddly different, more like a cry of distress, a warning; or a combination of the two. A distress call that Coyote and I had entered into someone's sacred circle uninvited and a warning that we should immediately stop and turn around.

I shouted: *"Did you hear that? What is it? I have never heard such a sound in my life. Look at me, my hair is standing straight up and my knees are shaking."*

Coyote: *"Marcus, you know I don't scare easily, but I believe I just wet myself."*

I exclaimed: *"There it is again! I think we should turn around and get the hell out of here!"*

I continued: *"Could these be the creatures the southern tribes had warned me about? Are these the monsters of the*

5

forest that steal and eat the children? Could they be the ones who are almost human but much, much larger and ten times as viscous; the ones that pick their teeth with the bones of their prey? The ones they call the Yeti, who dip their victims' eyeballs into bowls of blood and lick their fingers dry for dessert after they have eaten their blinded prey alive?"

Coyote: *"There you go again; believing the gibberish someone has handed down a thousand years ago; nonsense!"*

Coyote: *"Listen Marcus, we haven't eaten anything since we left the Sierra Nevada Mountains five days ago. If we turn around now we might not make it back to safety. It's probably a bluff, a small harmless creature whose weird howl saves it from predators. You know how Nature is, she gives creatures all kinds of gadgets and tricks to help them save themselves from the meat eaters, us; well I mean you. This is most likely a small bird with enormous vocal cords; just another trick of Nature. You know how she likes to toy with us."*

The howling stopped and the forest went silent. Even the breeze and the natural movements and sounds of the forest ceased; for the moment a silent pause in a frozen landscape.

Coyote: *"Let's get moving and put some distance between us and that awful sound. Move it little one and quicken your pace so we can get the hell away from here."*

Coyote convinced me to continue our trek on the trail. Late into the night we found level ground and made camp. By this time we were ravenous.

Along the trail Coyote and I found some wild looking mushrooms. Against our better judgement and with nothing else to eat, we eagerly ate the sweet tasting mushrooms. After eating the mushrooms we laid down to sleep. Scared, I curled up next to Coyote and we settled in for the night. Just as we closed our eyes and began to drift, it started. There it was the knocking on the trees and the dreaded feeling that something evil was watching us. We abruptly woke up.

Out there in the blackness of the forest something dark and sinister; something horrible and threatening was watching us. Before Coyote could blink, I found myself under his feet shaking like a leaf.

I said loudly: *"WTF was that? Did you hear that?"*

Shaking himself, Coyote responded: *"Settle down little brother. I won't let anything hurt you!"*

The knocking was methodical; knock---knock---knock, a pause, then two knocks close to each other; knock-knock. They had us surrounded. From the blackness of the forest the unnerving knocks and subtle grunts continued.

In an attempt to frighten the thing in the forest away, Coyote let out a howl directed at the source of the knocking and unfamiliar grunts. Out of the blackness came a broken branch hurtling through the air striking Coyote in his hindquarters knocking him off of his feet. Coyote yelped in pain.

The knocking stopped and voices came from the forest that could be seen but not heard. It was scripted in the language of the Earth that all but the humans could read.

The forest echoed with many voices: *"We are watching you; **watching you, watching you.** Beware we are watching you; **watching you, watching you.** You have entered our forest without our permission; **our permission, permission, permission.** Beware and turn back before it's too late; **too late, too late.** We are hungry and need to feed; **to feed, to feed.** Our babies are hungry and must have something to eat; **to eat, to eat.** The nights belong to us; **to us, to us.** We feed on your darkness and fear; **darkness and fear, and fear."***

The Path of the Spirit Walkers

After a brief pause a strong voice emerged from the forest: *"My name is Rahoo. I am the chief of my clan. We are the Spirit Walkers. We are the ones who protect the forest. We have come to measure your threat against Nature."*

"We are the children and the people of the forest. We are one with Nature and walk in balance and harmony with her. We are born to an extended family that wander near and far to tend to the wild. There are many of us but we only reveal ourselves to a few. There is no social order in our clan we all are equal. The title chief only means that I am the eldest of our clan."

"We celebrate birth, life, and death. We are born to our mate; the next male in birth is wedded to the next female in birth not of his immediate family. Together they play as brother and sister until they mature. This close bond joins them as equals. They are separated at maturity to wander the forest alone until they find each other again. Until that moment they are alone and sad for each other's love and company. They yearn for each other in a new way; not as brother and sister, but as young and eager lovers."

8

"This longing turns into a passion that ignites their senses. They can smell and taste each other over great distances. Their cravings drive them wild. They sing songs to each other and whisper love words into the wind that can only be heard in their private souls. In their dreams they kiss."

"They are intensely connected to each other and cry out at night their pain and eagerness to be together. They leave their scent for the other to find. At the passing of each day the circle that separates them grows smaller and smaller. They are close enough to touch; but frightened, he evades."

"The females take the lead and track their mates down. The males are bewildered and do not completely understand the rise of their passions. They have been transformed into a throbbing mess and don't quite know what to do. The females take them in hand and gently guide them home."

"The females are determined and soon the two are joined as one and remain so for months. With great joy the male quickly learns and their passions rage on throughout their joyful lives; together as one, never leaving the other's side. In love they are wedded; him to her and her to him."

"They are together from birth as brother and sister, together in life as loving mates and together in the twilight as friends; they are joined forever in love until their reunion with Nature rejoins them in death. The circle of circles finally closes with their souls joined forever as one with the Earth."

Rahoo continued: *"Nature's bounty is measured. Keeping the balance we limit the birth of our children to two; one each to replace ourselves. Only if we lose a child will we have another, keeping this balance."*

"As soon as the child is conceived both parents know. The male is on double duty to care for and protect the female. He announces their joy to the clan and makes offerings of thanks to Nature. He is at her side always and unselfishly takes care of her. The child is born into his hands. He is the first to kiss and present this gift to the world. He washes the newborn in a wild stream to bless the child's journey through life. In its birth he finds meaning and purpose. In giving life they (we) are born again."

Silently by Rahoo's side stood Hoora his mate for life.

The Marriage of Rahoo and Hoora

Like all the Spirit Walkers before them, at conception Rahoo and Hoora were joined forever as one. Once they found each other, their honeymoon lasted six lunar cycles; from six new moons until six full moons. They were joined as one during this cycle only separating to forage for food and water. They exhausted themselves with love. Their passions filled the forest with the sounds of love; soft whispers and gentle kisses. The joyful sounds only lovers know. The wild things were listening and giggled with delight. Rahoo's and Hoora's need to touch and kiss was without bounds. When parted they raced back to each other for more.

After their wild union they slowly wandered home to announce their new child to be. They journeyed home to his clan and he presented his new wife, their adopted daughter. Hoora was embraced for the second time not as a little sister for Rahoo, but as his wife.

Throughout the forest their story was carried in the wind. Clans from the hinterlands were called forward to celebrate their marriage. A great feast and ceremony honoring their union filled the camp with joy. Blooms were gathered to cover the bride and groom.

The tribe's elders, Crilu and Lucri presented Rahoo's and Hoora's tokens of love to each other. The joys and sufferings of life were to be shared and carried equally by the newly joined couple. For her a majestic butterfly was given to adorn her beauty, for him a thorn to remind him of the pain she would suffer for their love. The whole tribe quietly watched as their tears moistened the air.

Rahoo kneeled and begged for her love: *"Will you love me as I love you until death do us part and through death we will be rejoined forever as one with the Earth? I will be by your side forever to protect and honor you my sister and my wife."*

Given to him by Rahoo, Crilu placed the butterfly on Hoora's left shoulder reminding her and the tribe that Rahoo would always be at her side to protect and care for her. Resting for a moment the butterfly paused then flew off into the forest; carried by the wind into the unknown.

Hoora: *"Yes I will love you until my heart no longer beats. I will meet you in the hereafter joined together forever with the Earth. I will carry and bear our children and care for you each moment of my life. What Nature has given me, life, I will give to you. She is our Mother and through her we were born. I am now her daughter, your sister and your wife."*

Given the thorn by Hoora, Lucri holding Rahoo's right hand, jabbed the torn deep into his palm to remind him of the births Hoora would suffer for their love. Wrapped with wild vines; her left hand held in his right hand; they were joined as one, bound together forever by love.

The members of the tribe sang and danced with happiness for the newly married couple; around and around they danced until the sun broke through the trees and the dawn of the new day illuminated their joy.

Being invisible, Coyote and Marcus did not know Hoora, Rahoo's wife was quietly standing by his side hiding in the forest.

The Teachings of Nature

Rahoo: *"The forest has taught us everything we know. Nature speaks to us in words that are scripted by her own hands: "Harmony and Balance, Reverence for all that is Nature." Only those who seek her truths will find and read these sacred words; words without time, time without words."*

"She has fashioned the world around us; the force of the wind, the currents in the seas, every blade of grass, every leaf, every tree and every frog. All that crawls, swims or flies belong to her, the Sun and the Moon, every star; the Cosmos itself. She is time infinite and beyond, and even before. She is the Universe and all of the yesterdays and tomorrows are hers'."

"She formed the cliffs that surround us in the canyons, the mountains that reach into the skies and their snow covered peaks, the driest desert, a drop of water and the oceans, the

human hand, all created and fashioned in her light and in her way."

Purity of Being

Rahoo: *"Throughout life we, the Spirit Walkers tend to the wild. We are the gardeners of the forest. Our bodies have evolved to absorb the nutrients of the plants we eat leaving their seeds intact. When the seeds pass from our bodies we carefully cultivate these enriched seeds back into the Earth. We take great care not to reveal our work to others gently working the wild seeds back into the soil leaving the surroundings undisturbed."*

"We care for the wild things. We tend to the innocent, weak and sickly when we can. At times Nature intercedes and we must always yield to her wisdom."

"Our way of life is filled with Nature's rich bounty and our internal peace allows many of us to live beyond a thousand years. In this time we grow old with goodness and wisdom. We bring no harm to ourselves or those we love."

"We seek purity of being in that we lust for nothing and rejoice in contentment and balance. We walk in harmony and grace with Mother Earth. Our reunion back to the Earth completes our circle; birth - death, with life in between."

The Little Ones

Rahoo: *"Because we are not meat eaters the little ones, the opossums, rabbits, raccoons, and the other small furry ones; those that cannot readily defend themselves or escape the humans, seek our shelter. They and their families join us in our hiding places. The little ones often follow us on our migrations from one feeding place to another."*

The Invisible

Rahoo: *"We are careful to leave no signs for the humans to follow or to know that we exist. We seldom reveal even the slightest glimpse of ourselves to keep them fearful of us and confused. They have lied as to what they have found of us and who we truly are."*

"The hair we shed dissolves with the slightest moisture without a trace. Because of our life long herbal diets our bodies decompose within minutes after we die including our bones and teeth."

"We are the Spirit Walkers whose footsteps barely touch the ground let alone leave a footprint. The humans that say they have found evidence of our existence are not telling the truth and those that claim that they have seen us are delusional or liars."

"We take great care during the day not to be seen only revealing a glimpse of ourselves as we rapidly move through the forest or late at night while hiding within the shadows."

"We reveal ourselves only to scare the many or reward the few. We attempt to scare the many who are trying to hunt us down. We reveal ourselves to the few who are trying to be the good keepers of this Earth."

"Yes we are the Spirit Walkers whose foot prints leave no impressions on the ground. Only when we choose to leave signs or present a glimpse of ourselves to the few, do we

reveal ourselves or leave tracks. We temporarily leave our prints to scare or fool the humans who don't respect Nature. The humans call us the Yeti. **The humans are coming!"**

The Humans

Rahoo: *"In the future the humans who cannot read the signs of the Earth will recklessly cut down the forest. Trees that stood for hundreds of years will perish overnight. The homes of thousands of animals will disappear. All the animals that relied on the forest for food and shelter will also perish. For profit and greed these woodlands will vanish."*

*"If the humans don't change their ways they will bring darkness to the Earth. **Beware, the humans are coming!"***

"If humans could capture our DNA it would confirm our lineage tied directly to them and that they are members of our family and that in fact we are their elders."

"The humans have made up hundreds of stories as to our existence, not one of which is the truth. These lies have spread all over the world and have landed here."

"They call us the Yeti (Big Foot – Sasquatch) and describe us as blood thirsty villains to scare their little ones. We are in truth more humane then the humans. They have killed thousands upon thousands of their own. We have never taken the life of one of our own and only engage in violence to protect our loved ones."

"They spread horrible lies that we steal and eat their children and elderly, when the opposite is true. In the early years the humans often discarded their elderly and

15

abandoned them on the trail as the rest of the tribe moved on. They left their elderly in the forest to die alone. Some humans are so wicked and selfish that they even abandon their own children."

"We took pity on these poor souls, took them in and cared for them. The children we would raise until their fifth year, releasing them into the wild to find their way home. The elderly we nursed until they passed. Then we carefully returned their bodies to the Earth."

"For the special few; the lost children, the abandoned elderly or the keepers, in friendship we walk naked in their presence. Then we use herbs to carefully wash their memories away to protect our image. Only in their dreams do we visit them to reaffirm our love and friendship."

"To the children that fate left with us and the elderly who pass our way into the unknown, we stay forever faithful. We reveal ourselves to these few. To the others we stay elusive, unseen and invisible."

"You have nothing to fear. We are the gardeners of the forest. We have chosen to be with Nature and walk her narrow trails."

The Great Darkness

Rahoo: *"A long time ago when we were much younger as a species the world we know trembled beneath our feet. This tremor lasted for days and seemed to originate from horizon to horizon. The Earth shook and rumbled as if it was breaking apart."*

"The days grew darker and darker and the sky grew dense with ash. It took months for the ash to settle and the skies to slowly clear. The total blackness lasted several weeks and the Earth grew very cold. We took refuge in the caves where we stored our extra food and kept our fires going to keep us warm. Yes, we borrowed fire from Nature first then shared our discovery with the humans."

"It took months for the skies to clear and the Earth to return into the light. The black skies slowly turned dark grey, and the grey slowly turned blue and the rain clouds slowly scrubbed the skies clean of the ash. By this time thousands of species had disappeared. Those relying on meat starved."

"In the far east across the ocean of oceans the humans, our younger siblings, were extremely reckless and did not plan beyond each day. They relied on the meat of animals and a few plants to sustain themselves. They were primarily scavengers with very poor hunting skills and limited night vision. They were caught unprepared to last out the darkness."

"Only one skinny and starving tribe of humans survived. They had observed our gentle and generous natures and came to us for help. They were our baby brothers and sisters, they made their way to us and of course we took them in."

"Unlike the humans we are nocturnal. During the day we take refuge in our secrete places to take long naps and care for each other. We are vegetarians with an abundance of food sources to draw from. We had grown accustomed not to rely on one source and to store our food carefully away for the long winters."

"With the daylight returning we shared our food with the humans who greedily ate more than they needed laying around for hours trying to recover from each meal. They are gluttonous and we allowed them to eat their fill. They have many vices and constantly fuss and fight with each other."

"It was nearly a total extinction but enough of us survived to carry on. The animal kingdom very slowly regained its hold on life and the humans abruptly left us to recover their claim on the lands that surrounded us."

Out of Africa / The Spirit Walkers

Rahoo: *"Like the humans the Spirit Walkers evolved from the "knuckle walkers" the great apes that inhabited the highland forests and jungles of Africa. A group of these great apes, our forbearers, gradually moved down into the lowlands and into the surrounding savannas."*

"There, these "pre-humans" found new challenges for survival. Unlike the great apes they began to walk on two legs and use their forelimbs and hands to reach up into the stunted trees bearing fruits, berries and nuts for nourishment. Paired with scavenging they began to prosper and readily mastered their new niche."

"Standing erect and with the use of their hands they/we became very successful; challenging the survival of the other wild creatures that once dominated the savannas."

"In one savanna stood a special tree, known by the wild ones as the Tree of Life. Located on a small patch of ground it was surrounded by bedrock where nothing else grew. This

exposed bedrock stretched out in every direction from this tree for hundreds of feet."

"Reaching the fruit of this unique tree proved to be extremely difficult. The Tree of Life rose out of the ground with a trunk rising twelve feet before its branches began to span outward. The trunk of this tree was perfectly round and as hard and slick as polished granite. Even for the pre-humans the Tree of Life was impossible to climb."

"This tree bared the richest fruit on the Earth. This fruit resembled a mango in its size, outer skin and shape, with the fruit itself having the texture of a ripe peach. Each fruit's color was unique revealing color blends of: blue, green, red, yellow, copper, gold, turquois, pink, purple,,,,. Each fruit swirled in colors without end. Although limited in the number of fruit, the Tree of Life yielded fruit year around."

"The nourishment of just one fruit from the Tree of Life could sustain a large creature for days. Its possession was the envy of many; but the prize of only a few."

"Only a few of the pre-humans could leap and reach these precious fruits. Coupled with great strength and larger, leaner bodies a small number of them were able to jump high enough to reach and snatch the tree's treasured gifts. These pre-humans mated with each other and within a short span of a few thousand years stood over nine feet tall and could leap up and climb into the Tree of Life itself."

"Being generous by Nature the taller pre-humans shared what they could with the short ones. The short ones were never satisfied and complained bitterly."

"The other pre-humans soon became jealous of the tall ones and rejected them from their tribe. Once the shorter "humans" mastered tool making they created the ax, and for spite chopped down the Tree of Life. Those that cut it down fed on her fruit for one day. The tree named Eve, that fed thousands over the years, was gone forever."

"Given their mean and vulgar ways the smaller pre-humans teased and taunted the larger pre-humans driving them out of Africa into the northeastern deserts. Deprived of their sacred tree for nourishment the tall ones in desperation fled the savanna in search for food. We walked for thousands and thousands of miles."

"We the Spirit Walkers started our own tribe and pledged fidelity with Nature promising to never take more than what we truly needed. Once beyond the deserts in search of peace and harmony we journeyed deeper and deeper into the great eastern forest that stretched across Asia to the Pacific Ocean."

"Driven by their selfish wants the humans were always invading and destroying the forest. We attempted to frighten them away by disguising ourselves as hideous monsters and in return they told horrible stories about our beings."

"Justifying their fear and hatred for us they constantly hunted us down. The humans took one of our little boys and treated him cruelly for years. He finally escaped and formed an alliance with the other wild ones to defeat the humans in a great battle. This battle was recorded in our ancient writings; words without paper,"

"In spite of his faith and love for all that is Nature, this Spirit Walker became a great warrior in the defense of his people and the little ones who became our friends; the enemies of our enemies are indeed our friends."

*"The little ones would become our eyes and ears. Whenever the humans threatened the wellbeing, peace and tranquility of the forest, their calls, cries and wild noises would alert us of the danger. They were forever watching letting us know that the humans were coming, **were coming, coming.**"*

The Struggle

Rahoo: *"There was a time when we lived in the open with the humans. We evolved about four millions years ago eons before the rise of the humans. We joyfully lived in harmony with the natural world. We decided early on to be in balance with Nature and live within her margins; birth and death with life in between. For generations we and the humans lived side by side sharing the bounty of Nature in peace."*

"The humans unlike us had many children; with dozens of children being born within one family. Their numbers grew tenfold times tenfold. Once they started to cultivate the land they became quarrelsome with each other and at odds with Nature. They began to challenge us for the forest."

"They soon forgot our kindness during the great darkness and began to hunt us down. They prided themselves for being hairless, naked apes, and spread lies as to our true natures. They used our hairy bodies to turn us into monsters. Our red hair scared them. They were told by their parents, from generation to generation, that the red color in our hair was drawn from the blood of our victims; which is a lie. Our red

hair comes from the blend of herbs and roots we regularly eat and has become part of our being through time."

"They began to tell stories that we were monsters; fierce demons that hunt and kill the weak. They said we were the creatures of the night that preyed on the helpless. And that our souls are filled with darkness and evil, and our minds have been corrupted by our wicked thoughts and deeds."

"Just the opposite is true. We are in harmony with all life forms and respect the creatures of the Earth. We tend the forest and do what we can to preserve the wild things. We have decided not to challenge Nature but rather to embrace her and follow her natural rhythms. We are the good stewards of the land and life. We are content to live within the bounds of Nature and for that the humans despise us."

"All the animals in the forest are our brothers and sisters. We do not eat meat. We eat only the vegetation Nature provides. You can find food everywhere in the forest if you know where to look and what to eat."

"We eat the roots and berries and many of the green plants and most of the mushrooms found on the forest floor and in the trees. With the mushrooms you must take care not to eat the striped sweet ones; they can mess with your minds."

"We move constantly from one location to another. We never eat more than we need and take care not to over graze in any one location. We are one with Nature and return nutrients to the soils keeping the needs of the forest in balance with the needs of ourselves and the other creatures that rely on the Earth for their lives."

22

"Sadly the humans can't read the signs of the Earth and will not hear or see this message. They can't comprehend contentment and balance. They are wasteful and greedily devour the Earth's natural resources. They will take what they want and steal from others. They are selfish and lustful; corrupted by their own sense of sin. They are at odds with the natural systems that sustain life on this planet."

The Great Escape

Rahoo: *"In the east the humans made war on our kind driving us into extinction in Africa, Europe and Asia. During this violent conflict a few of us escaped across the ice bridge that stretched from Siberia to Alaska."*

"After we saved them and gave them fire they turned on us as they had turned on Nature. As their lust for land and possessions grew they became more and more heartless, selfish and violent. They invaded the forest with their weapons of stone and attacked us. We withdrew deeper into the forest to our hiding places."

"They hunted us down and killed many of our kind taking the children captive. A few of them pleaded with their leaders to spare the children. The controlling elite would have none of it stating they could not bear to live with the little hairy ones and they killed all of our captured babies."

"At the "narrows" a small band of our fathers stood against a large army sent to destroy us. In the struggle the ice bridge cracked and broke apart sending our fathers and the attacking humans to their deaths."

The Ice Bridge

Rahoo: *"I was just a boy when word came that the human army was getting closer to our camp. Kralu the eldest of the tribe assembled the fathers stating that some of them would have to stay behind to stop the humans from crossing the ice bridge to the Americas. The only hope for escape was to make a stand."*

Kralu: *"We must stand our ground and sacrifice our lives. We must destroy the ice bridge before the humans get here. Some of the fathers will build a wall to hold them back while the rest of the fathers and mothers destroy the bridge behind us and help the tribe and our families to escape."*

Rahoo: *"Kralu said we would have to break with tradition this one time to save the tribe. Some fathers and mothers would have to leave each other for the first time since the beginning of time."*

Rahoo: *"While the ice bridge was being destroyed Kralu's wife, Lukra would lead the rest of the tribe across the ice into the unknown; the great wilderness. She now would lead the tribe to safety."*

Rahoo: *"Husbands kissed their wives goodbye and brothers kissed sisters. The children held firmly to their father's legs and cried. Desperately clinging to their fathers, mothers had to pull their grief stricken children away. Tears froze to their fathers' cheeks while they waved farewell to their families. With determination the fathers and some of the mothers turned to face the humans."*

Rahoo: *"My mother grabbed my hand and clutched my baby sister against her breast and turned away. With tears washing down her face she waved farewell to our father for the last time. Our father blew kisses into the air saying goodbye to my mother and his babies."*

Rahoo: *"The humans were vicious and would spare none of us. They had tracked us down and were gaining ground slowly closing the gap between us. If they caught us in the open they would kill us all."*

Kralu said: *"We will make our stand at the "narrows" where the ice bridge is only ninety meters wide and the ocean current below is most swift. While the majority of us build and defend the wall, the remaining fathers and mothers will begin to weaken the exposed crevasse."*

Kralu continued: *"No matter what is taking place at the wall, those weakening the ice bridge must not stop. We can only hold them back for a while. Their army is too large to defeat."*

Kralu again: *"The ice bridge must be broken no matter what is happening at the wall."*

Kralu to Luway his trusted friend: *"You must ensure that no one working on the crevasse leaves their post. If the bridge breaks you must leave us behind and catch up with the tribe and your families."*

Kralu: *"NO MATTER WHAT HAPPENS THE ICE BRIDGE MUST BE DESTROYED!"*

Rahoo: *"They used the stone tools captured from the humans to cut the blocks of ice. They formed teams and quickly built an ice wall fifteen feet high and ten feet wide. They began to stack additional ice blocks on top of the wall to hurl down on the humans."*

Rahoo: *"Up on the wall our fathers were completely exposed to the human stone tipped weapons."*

Rahoo: *"If our fathers failed to stop the humans we had to make it to the wild lands and vanish into the forest."*

Kralu: *"Once the ice bridge collapses the ocean current will wash the remaining ice away. The tribe must quickly make it to the other side and go into hiding until those of us who survive can catch up."*

Rahoo: *"A winter storm raged in front of us. Lukra guided the tribe straight into the raging blizzard. The ice and snow was blinding. We clutched onto those in front of us to keep our bearings and stay together. We held firmly to each other as we moved forward into the blinding snow. Lukra led us deeper into the blizzard to hide our tracks in case the humans defeated our fathers and made it across the ice bridge. Leaving our fathers and some of our mothers behind, we vanished into the storm."*

Rahoo: *"At the "narrows" our fathers and a few mothers began to break away the ice and build the wall. Once the wall was completed three hundred of our fathers posted themselves on top of the wall to face the enemy. In the thousands the humans formed up. Restricted by the "narrows" only a few hundred of the enemy could attack the wall at a time."*

Rahoo: *"While the three hundred defended the wall the work teams deepened the crevasse sending blocks of ice forward to the Spirit Walkers manning the wall. The crevasse grew deeper and deeper. Word came forward that the work teams could hear the ocean moving below and the ice bridge was beginning to give way."*

Kralu sent word to the work teams: *"DO NOT STOP DIGGING THROUGH THE ICE. IT MUST GIVE WAY!"*

Kralu: *"Once the ice breaks save as many of yourselves as you can and make it back to the tribe and your families. Protect them with your lives. I love you and will carry your spirits with me into the unknown."*

The Wall

Rahoo: *"Our fathers took their positions on the wall each behind a stack of ice blocks. The human army moved forward pushing many of their own warriors against the wall. The humans threw spears and fired arrows at our fathers. The height of the wall matched by the strength of our fathers stopped the army in its tracks."*

Rahoo: *"As the humans gathered at the base of the wall they were crushed to death by the army behind them and the ice blocks hurled down upon them by our fathers. The surface below the wall quickly turned red with their blood staining the ice surrounding the "narrows."*

Rahoo: *"The pile of dead humans in front of the wall grew higher and higher. Our fathers fought frantically to keep the humans from climbing over the bodies of their fellow warriors up onto the wall. When the humans finally* breached the wall our fathers grabbed them up like broken dolls and tossed them to the ground below."

Rahoo: *"Wounded by many spears and arrows our fathers fought on. A great struggle between life and death took place on top of the wall. Our fathers fought desperately to keep the humans back. One by one our fathers began to fall. Kralu and his last few warriors stood fast and fought off wave after wave of the attacking humans. My father was with him when Kralu fell. The last of our fathers were soon overwhelmed."*

Rahoo: *"Then the ice bridge shuttered. The wall shook from end to end. A great cracking sound traveled forward from the crevasse to the top and base of the wall and throughout the "narrows" itself. The wall tilted forward, then backward and began to crumble. The "narrows" and the ice bridge began to shatter and fall apart. The great Artic Ocean spilled over the fallen wall and crumbling ice bridge washing them into the Pacific Ocean. Into this swirl the humans and our fathers were swept away. With a great rush the wall and the ice bridge collapsed and disappeared."*

Rahoo: *"Only one wounded Spirit Walker survived the collapse of the wall and the breaking apart of the ice bridge to tell this story. Nearly frozen to death he made it across the "narrows" carried on the back of a majestic sea turtle. Her name was Florence and she told him her story. She was the mother of King Kamehameha of the beautiful Hawaiian Islands; the Garden before Eden. She carried the warmth of these tropical islands with her slowly bringing this wounded Spirit Walker back to life. Safely crossing the "narrows" she set him ashore and wished him well. Mother Nature had warmed the Artic waters and saved his life. My father was spared by Happenchance and delivered back to his family.*

28

Out of the blizzard his spirit walked back into our presence and returned to his loving and grateful family."

Rahoo: *"Those of us who escaped over the ice bridge were the last to survive and vowed never to fully trust the humans again. We took a sacred oath to only reveal ourselves to the children, sick or elderly and in rare cases, a keeper or two."*

Rahoo: *"We will protect ourselves and our children and try hard to scare the humans away, but we don't seek to kill or harm others. Only when we are threatened will we engage in mortal defense. We are the keepers of the forest. Beware, the humans are coming, **are coming, are coming!**"*

David and Golith

Rahoo: *"Many of the little ones escaped across the ice bridge with us. One was a raccoon named David. Knowing the humans well, David escaped across the ice bridge with his entire tribe and his friends, the Spirit Walkers."*

Rahoo: *"When David was a young warrior his tribe was at war with the humans. The humans were mesmerized with the raccoon's fur and designed caps made from their hides and tails. These "coon-skin-caps" brought great prices in their market places along with the stolen wild children and the meat from the other wild beings that lived in the forest."*

Rahoo: *"David was called by his king to unite the wild ones and lead an army against the humans to stop this deadly practice before all the wild beings were driven into extinction. In response, the humans "summoned" a giant from the forest, using this giant to threaten and destroy the king's army."*

Rahoo: *"David had heard two stories about this giant. One was that the giant was a foul smelling monster from the deep forest of Siberia who was the greatest warrior that ever lived. It was told by the humans that Golith enjoyed killing his enemies, eating them while they were still alive. He would take many bites casting his prey aside to die while he attacked and ate the next victim in line. He craved blood and flesh and smeared the remains of his enemies all over his massive body. Suffering many wounds he never was defeated or withdrew; winning many battles for the humans."*

Rahoo: *"The second story claimed that this giant belonged to a family of gentle creatures. They were the only humans who never left the forest and held a deep spiritual regard for Nature and all living things. They and we are known as the Spirit Walkers, the guardians of the forest and wild things. We only defend ourselves when attacked or to protect the innocent and our loved ones. Golith was one of us."*

Rahoo: *"Pretending an attack the humans mustered their army in front of David's fortifications. The humans used this opportunity to parade Golith in front of David's army. Golith was heavily armored with sharp metal spikes protruding forward from his helmet. His battle dress included long coarse red hair that covered his entire body. He carried a great battle ax and was smeared with blood. He beat his battle ax against his shield and released a bone shattering scream. All the goats in the fields fell dead. Many in David's army began to shake and cry."*

Rahoo: *"David faced Golith, boldly stood his ground and quietly calmed his fellow warriors. David declared: 'I will defeat this monster tomorrow."*

Rahoo: *"After a few moments the humans withdrew believing Golith had put fear into the hearts of David's army for the upcoming battle. The humans believed David's army would quit the field and scatter once Golith appeared on the field again.*

Rahoo: *"The humans sent word to David and challenged him to stand alone against Golith."*

Rahoo: *"That evening David consulted with his commanders. To a warrior they recommended that their army withdraw; that there was no possible way to defeat this monster and the human army. If they stood against Golith, tomorrow they would all be slaughtered."*

Rahoo: *"David was deeply trouble by his commanders' advice. What if the story about the gentle nature of this giant was true; that he was a Spirit Walker, a guardian of the forest who reveres life? What would motivate Golith to take sides with the humans? David knew something was wrong."*

Rahoo: *"That night David disguised himself as a merchant and entered his enemy's camp. David soon discovered that Golith was not welcomed in the humans' camp and was left in the forest to camp alone. Golith's fire drew David to his side. From the darkness of the forest David spoke to Golith in a voice that could be seen but not heard. Like all wild things Golith recognized the words; the voice of Nature."*

David: *"I am David, leader of the wild things that will stand against you in battle tomorrow. Although human like in form, you are a wild one like us. You still live in the forest and speak our language. Why do you fight against us tomorrow?"*

Golith: *"You know I could eat you in a blink. You are very brave or very foolish to come here tonight. I believe it must be bravery and goodness that brings you here. I will listen and see your words."*

David again: *"Why do you fight against your own kind, your extended family tomorrow?"*

Golith: *"The humans have my wife and babies locked up in cages deep within a secret cave. They have threatened to roast them alive if I do not stand against you in battle. They are arrogant and cruel without a soul or conscience when it comes to those of us from the wild. They will kill us for trophies and skins and leave our bodies to rot."*

Rahoo: *"David was astonished how handsome Golith was. Although heavily scarred and covered with very fine soft red hair he was the most perfect looking human he had ever seen. Standing well over nine feet tall his muscular body was massive and gifted with agility in every move. He had one blue eye and one green eye with pupils as big as quarters; the gentle light within his soul radiated wonder and affection. He was not the monster he appeared to be; a lie fanned by the humans to bring fear into the hearts of others.*

Rahoo: *"Golith told David that he was just a baby when he was captured. The humans kept him in a cage of steel and fed him raw garbage crawling with flies and bugs. They beat him daily making him very angry inside. The humans would match him up with lions and bears in an arena to teach him to kill and to further build up his strength. The humans would wage on the winner and would often match Golith against three or more bears or lions at a time.*

Rahoo continued: *"Golith shared that one night his cruel keeper became drunk and passed out next to his cage. Golith took the keys from the keeper's belt and in rage woke the keeper up."*

Rahoo: *"Golith said to his keeper;* **'I have your keys; see if any of you escape me now."**

Rahoo: *"Golith in a blind rage freed himself from the cage and killed all the humans in his path to freedom and escaped into the Siberian Forest. He heard her cries in the forest and was finally reunited with his lifelong mate; with their love and the births of their children, peace returned to his heart."*

Rahoo: *"Years later Golith's family was captured by the humans and held as hostages. Golith was forced to fight in the human wars disguised as a monster to frighten their enemies. Torn, he was condemned to a life of misery."*

David to Golith: *"I promise this nightmare is over. Tomorrow when you face us a green flag will mean that your wife and children have been set free and are in our camp safe and well; ready to be with you again."*

David: *"I have disguised myself as a merchant. My merchandize is some very strong whiskey that loosens tongs. I have left two goat skins full of whiskey with the chief scout who promised to take me to the cave to see the red monsters for an extra skin of whiskey."*

David: *"I will locate the cave, get the fools drunk and free your wife and babies. Look carefully under the green flag between the barriers, you will recognize the eyes and faces of your family."*

33

David: *"No matter what the outcome tomorrow, your family will be set free and returned to your people. This I promise."*

David: *"If I fail in my mission you are free to take my life."*

David: *"You must stand before me and fiercely contest my presence. I will face you with my sling and score a direct strike to your forehead with a plum instead of a stone. You will grasp your head and fall to the ground pretending death. You will make a terrible cry as you fall to the Earth. The humans will shout: 'Golith; the great warrior giant, killed by a single stone from David's sling."*

David: *"You will carry a goat skin full of human blood next to your body. After you fall I will take a sharpen stick and viciously stab the goat skin several times pretending to ensure your death, spilling "your blood" onto the ground. I will scream victory and my army will pour out of our fortress."*

David: *"You must trust me!"*

David: *"If the trick works, the human army will fold, scatter and run for their lives. If not, you will rise and stand with us against the humans."*

Rahoo: *"David and Golith met in the open field of battle and acted out their roles. The armies formed and in the middle of the field David "slew" Golith. The humans, as expected, fled the field of battle. They could not believe that a raccoon with a sling and a stick could kill this mighty giant."*

Rahoo: *"After the battle, Golith and David became best friends. David and his tribe joined Golith's clan and they lived together for years. They journeyed deep into the great Siberian Forest and lived in peace following their oneness with Nature, the Mother of the Cosmos. Golith was one of the three hundred Spirit Walkers fighting the humans when the ice-bridge and the wall at the narrows collapsed."*

Free at Last

Rahoo: *"Once the little ones realized the new forest was free of the humans, they spread out across the Americas like fireflies some reaching the eastern woodlands as far away as the Atlantic Ocean. David's tribe settled along the Atlantic coast and for many years David honored us with his visits to our forest in the western mountains."*

Marcus to himself: *"Were these my ancestors. Was David my great, great, great grandfather? Could this be true, are we dreaming?"*

An Unforgiveable Future

Speaking to Coyote and I, a soft angelic voice echoed in the forest. The wind whispered: *"I am Hoora the first and only mate of Rahoo, **Rahoo, Rahoo…..** Our children's names are Ra and Hoo. They were born on my two hundred and fortieth full moon, during The Summer of Plenty. Their mates have yet to be born. Welcome to our treasured forest. May its beauty illuminate your hearts, and may contentment and balance be your guide.*

Hoora the Seer: *"The Earth as it now stands is threatened. The humans in the east, our half brothers and sisters, are out of control and mindlessly lust to destroy this planet. They are spreading their destruction around the world and are headed*

35

this way. *Like rabid termites they are devouring the woodlands.*"

Hoora the Seer: *"In the east across the great ocean the large animals and forest are disappearing. The smaller animals that rely on the forest are threatened. Life as we know it is slowly being corrupted."*

Hoora the Seer: *"In the future the humans will strip the land of its protective forest and pollute its waters. The soil will finally give out and the organic life within its protective cover will perish. Crops will fail and millions will die of starvation. Conflict will spread like the pox. Civil strife and war will break out everywhere."*

Hoora the Seer: *"Their machines will consume the Earth and all of its natural habitats. The humans will burn fossil fuels polluting the Earth's oceans and skies beyond repair. They will use chemicals on the land further contaminating the soil with toxins causing unhealthy mutations to life's basic structure, its DNA. These toxins will be washed out into the oceans further corrupting Nature's natural systems."*

Hoora the Seer: *"Before and after the deadly end reveals itself the atmosphere will continue to degrade. Climate change will be in full force by the year **2025** with America reaching temperatures of over one hundred fifteen degrees during its six months of summer. Fall and winter will last less than three months, with spring starting earlier each year ending by the middle of April. Spring temperatures at times will exceed one hundred degrees."*

Hoora the Seer: *"The western coast of North America will be ten feet underwater causing a massive migration of the* human population into the Sierra Nevada and Cascade Mountains to escape the rising sea level. Most of southern Florida will be covered by water, with the coastal cities and beaches around the Gulf of Mexico swallowed up by the oceans. Like a poisonous vapor fear will consume the masses."

Hoora the Seer: *"Slowly the humans will be pushed further and further inland stressing the Earth's natural systems to their breaking points. The wealthy will begin to build their shelters underground to escape the heat and madness generated by the shortage of clean air, food and water."*

Hoora the Seer: *"With the melting of the polar caps and glaciers, the loss of the coastal habitats will spread around the world. All the arid regions will intensify and become unfit for habitation. These waste lands will expand and begin to reach temperatures of one hundred fifty degrees. The dry regions will grow by over a million square miles creating a band of deserts around the world. The "green regions" will continue to shrink losing ground everywhere on the planet."*

Hoora the Seer: *"Too late, the human political systems will start to respond. All travel by their precious automobiles and air planes will be prohibited. The world will be placed on "lock down" as related to carbon dioxide emissions with radical steps toward sustainable green energy mandated by international law. All coal, petroleum and natural gas production will cease."*

Hoora the Seer: *"In 2030 zero impact on the environment will be mandated by their "United Nations" and everything produced by mankind must be recycled. The nations will make progress toward closing the landfills and cleaning up*

37

*the environment. The keepers will make strides politically and begin to have a positive impact on the movement toward a healthier ecosystem. Teetering on the **Eve of Destruction**, the Earth and our fates will hang in the balance."*

Hoora the Seer: *"The predictions are that by **2049** the flooding will finally peak at seventeen feet above the current sea levels. In the temperate zones the upper summer temperatures will reach one hundred thirty degrees."*

Hoora the Seer: *"Their science will be pushed to its limits and the greenhouse effect will appear to be reversing itself when the unimaginable happens. The biosphere will give rise to our worst nightmare. Our fates hang in the balance, **in the balance, the balance, the balance**...."*

Hoora the Seer: *"Marcus, one day soon your curiosity will put you at serious risk but a dark shadow will descend from the heavens to save you from certain death. She too has a warning to share that you must hear and keep for others. You have been chosen to record these visions and warn others of this coming doom."*

Hoora the Seer: *"For the time being we are here doing our best to protect the forest and the creatures it cares for. One way or the other, the future belongs to the humans."*

Rahoo: *"Coyote and Marcus, we sense no danger from you. It is clear you are wild ones too. Outside of this bluff you have nothing to fear from us. You are free to go."*

Rahoo's voice grew silent as he and his mate Hoora withdrew deeper into the forest. A quiet calm returned and the wilderness, which surrounded Coyote and I, reflected perfect peace. The threat was real only if the intruders were determined to bring ruin and destruction to their forest. The Spirit Walkers were there to keep the woodlands and wild things safe.

The Illusion

The next morning Coyote and I slowly woke to the reassuring chatter of the birds and were eager to get moving. Coyote insisted that we had a bad dream and if we searched the forest around us, we would find nothing.

I refused to budge: *"I am not going poking around in the forest! The stick that came flying at us last night and knocked you off your feet; it was real. There it is lying on the ground."*

Coyote: *"I am not bruised or injured. I tell you it was just a bad dream. You can wait here if you want, but I am going hunting for evidence to prove it was just a bad dream; fueled by the mushrooms and your overactive imagination; no evidence, no monsters!"*

Coyote ventured into the forest leaving Marcus alone on the trail. The deeper Coyote went the more convinced he was that it must have been the mushrooms. He rounded the last tree before he decided to turn around, and there they were pressed deeply within the moss; perfectly shaped footprints almost as if left there on purpose.

This creature left tracks larger than a bear's without any claws. Each print consisted of five small oblong impressions, with a hook shaped pad pressed beneath, followed by a deep oval shaped indentation. Each impression was over eighteen inches long from toes to heel. This two legged giant easily stood nine feet tall. The tracks were encased with signs of very coarse hair outlining each impression.

Coyote out loud: *"Could these tracks belong to the creatures that few have seen and that many keep talking about? Could these be the beings who told us their story last night; the Yeti, the Spirit Walkers?"*

Coyote said to himself: *"I feel a bit dizzy, am I still hallucinating from the mushrooms we ate? Could these foot prints be real? This cannot be."*

Coyote again to himself: *"I have never kept anything from Marcus before, but if I tell him about these tracks he will high tail it straight back to the Sierra Nevada Mountains. If we are going to go on and find the fire-mountains, I must not tell him what I have found. We have traveled too far to turn back now."*

A whisper quietly blew through the forest air; a gentle song with these tender lyrics moved through the trees and danced in Coyote's soul:

"We are here to protect the forest and remind others of their duties; to preserve this sacred Earth which has given us life. We live to live, we ponder to know, we grow wise to love and keep our balance with Nature. We are the Spirit Walkers, the keepers of the forest."

Coyote turned to take another look at the unusual tracks and in that instant the footprints had mysteriously disappeared. *"Damn those mushrooms!"* Coyote said out loud.

Back on the trail, Coyote claimed: *"I could not find a thing, not a hair, feces, the smell of urine, nothing; not a broken branch, turned up leaves or a footprint; absolutely nothing. It must have been the mushrooms. All is clear and it's safe to continue our trek to the fire-mountains."*

With blind faith Marcus took the lead and headed due north. They both wanted to forget the puzzling dream, get back on the trail and find the fire-mountains.

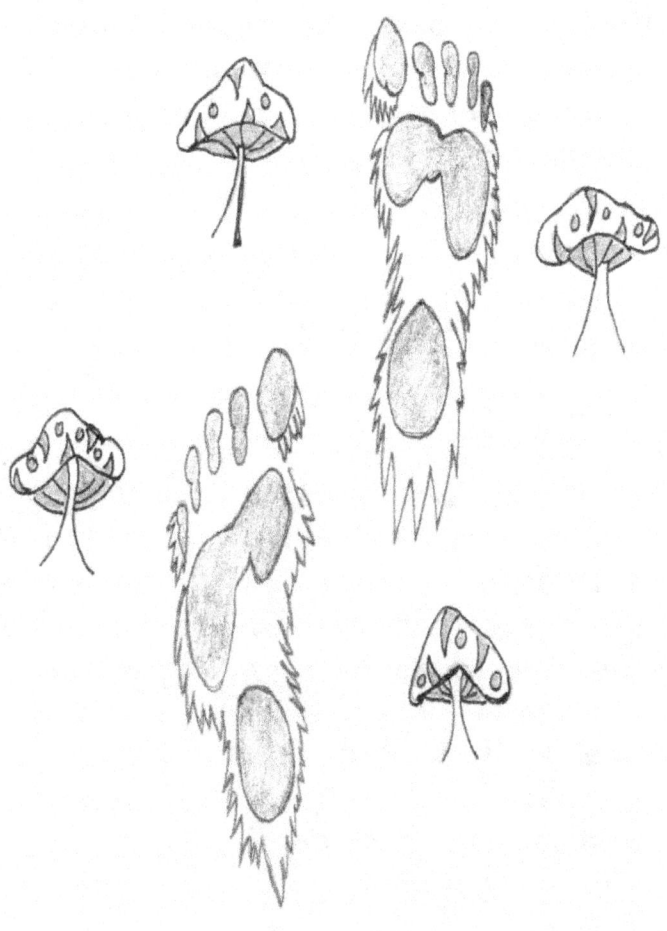

Unidentified Flying Objects

That night Coyote and I made camp higher up in the Cascade Mountains. Not fully recovered from the strange encounters and dreams we experienced the night before, we quietly settled in.

After a long and awkward silence, I began: *"Did you see that meteor last night, how it stopped in midflight and made that radical vertical turn? It looked like a flying disc!"*

I continued: *"I have never seen a meteor make a ninety degree vertical turn from a horizontal path before. It stopped abruptly in place and then flew straight up into the night sky and disappeared in a split second; impossible!"*

I asked: *"And did you see those bright flashing red and yellow orbs flying in different directions after hovering over our camp site? Again in a flash they were gone."*

Coyote: *"Marcus I am telling you it was those sweet mushrooms we ate. We were hallucinating. We were still tripping little guy, nothing else. All a figment of our imaginations and your over active exaggerations. Flashing orbs, vertical flight; you know how you expand the truth. Through those mushrooms we had entered the **Twilight Zone**; that place in our minds where we make things up."*

Coyote: *"Marcus, I saw that meteor and that was an air burst. That meteor just blew apart before it hit the Earth. And those orbiting lights were fireflies attracted to our camp site. I am telling you, you - we were hallucinating, just a bad trip little buddy. Like the one we had in the desert canyon years ago with the scorpion and cactus buttons.*

42

I stood my ground: *"I KNOW WHAT I SAW!"*

After another long pause, I pondered: *"Do you think living things can travel in space; that blackness that seems to extend forever above us? Do you think that space travel will be possible in the future?"*

Coyote: *"There are already creatures on Earth that have mastered flight; the eagle and the condor for example. We have been told that the humans are ingenious when it comes to making things; who knows they may in the future extend the mastery of flight into space travel."*

Coyote: *"But if those lights in the night's sky prove to be too far we might not be able to live long enough, or fly fast enough to make the journey to even the nearest star."*

Coyote: *"Space may prove to be an environment where living things, no matter how well protected, cannot long survive. We may someday travel to the moon and inhabit a planet or two, but space travel beyond our solar system may prove out of our grasp. In the end our physical limitations may prove too fragile for deep space."*

I agreed: *"We may find ourselves restricted to a narrow niche in which we can survive and prosper. Maybe the stars are too far. Once we reach our **Outer Limits** we will have to turn inward, to the Universe within ourselves, to find our true purpose and meaning."*

Coyote: *"Deep space; go where and for what purpose: to discover and destroy another planet, to drive thousands of other species into extinction? We need to comprehend and take care of what we have before we fly off into space."*

Coyote: *"Marcus, let's give our brains a rest. We had a pretty rough time of it last night. Let's give ourselves some quiet time. I have a lot on my mind right now, too much to worry about flying orbs and tree knockings."*

Farewell
Since our trek through the mushroom patch and our bizarre dreams about the Spirit Walkers and flying things, Coyote had been acting strange…

The Journey…..
This is just one of Marcus's many adventures. Meet all the characters and challenges Marcus faces in his quest for meaning and his journey across America.

<u>THE JOURNEY</u>
The Quest for Meaning – A Modern American Fable

<u>www.amazon.com/dp/0991502914</u>

This is a story about a young man's quest for meaning. He is a restless lad full of questions and hope. He seeks to know the world and leaves home at a young age to journey west. He defies his parents and leaves the protection of his family (the sacred circle – the protection of the mighty oak tree) to wander the Earth alone.

Through his travels he meets many characters; some who will lead him astray and others who will teach and guide him toward a *higher state of being*. There are the hollow ones, the spirit warriors, the controlling elite, the seekers-teachers-keepers and seers. He has dreams and visions and at times he is not certain if he is awake or asleep. The real world, he soon finds out, is often confusing with dreams and nightmares occurring both day and night. He discovers that we often disregard our dreams making the nightmares more real than they really are. And that we too often destroy what we build and pass the ruins of our destruction on to our children.

America at this time is not ready for the humans. It is the animal kingdom that will teach this young man his greatest lessons. He will fight in an unnecessary war and engage in criminal behavior. He will choose and live with bad company. There are those that will warn him about the coming future and the corruption of mankind in its callous relationship with the Earth. There are those that seek to destroy Marcus and those who will give their lives to protect him. He falls in love and has wonderful children and grandchildren. His wanderlust will lead him into the unknown. Chaos will pursue and catch up with him. He will be saved by the ones who love him the most.

He learns about the Universe and the natural wonder we call Earth. He gains a profound reverence for the Earth, our home, and ceases to believe in the gibberish handed down through the ages. He embraces the truth that we are of and from this Earth. He will discover the balance of Nature, the miracle of life and the inescapable reality of death. He will seek out and discover the unknown. His greatest teacher will be Nature herself.

His name is Marcus. He is a human who has disguised himself as a raccoon to better fit into the natural world. Although a good guy, he hides behind a mask to cover his true identity and misdeeds….. ***Where are you in terms of your state of being?*** In the quest for truth we seek knowledge and the acquisition of knowledge gains us wisdom. The highest state of being, a seer, is reserved for the few, but opened to all. Only those who are willing to travel far from home and learn through the passage of time become seers. Will you look within yourself and join Marcus on this journey? I warn you if we fail to find our way the world as we know it will be lost. There is a war going on; and that war is within ourselves.

Go To:

www.amazon.com/dp/0991502914

Also the Author of:

In the Shadows of the Dead / Vietnam 1968/69

This is a true story of an 18-19 year old U.S. Marine caught up in the Vietnam War. I was a machine gunner (M60) in Golf Company, 2nd Battalion, 26th Marines. I took part in Operations Meade River, Bold Mariner, Linn River and others. On January 28th, 1969 I had nine men killed within 20-30 meters of my gun position.

Go To:

www.amazon.com/dp/0991502922

"We Are Watching You!"
GGA

Eclipse
GGA

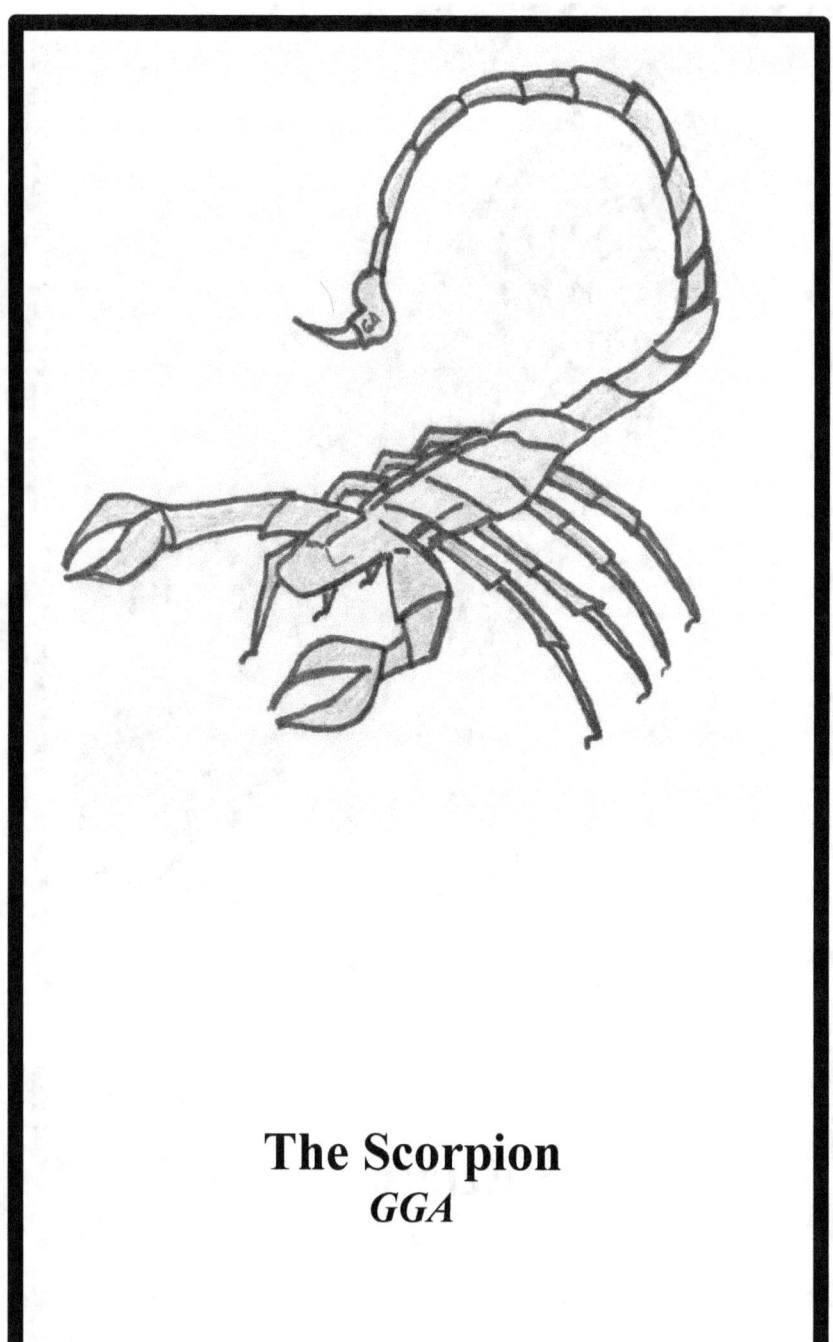

The Scorpion
GGA

THE JOURNEY
The Quest for Meaning

Coyote

Eternity/Infinity

Gila Monster

Scorpion

Survival

Midnight

Side Winder

Walking Moon

Eclipse

Chaos

Spirit Feather

Marcus

Seal

The Haversack

The Keeper

Happenchance

Justice

Jetta

Crazy Bear

Geo

Mother Condor

THE SACRED CIRCLE

www.ingramcontent.com/pod-product-compliance
Lightning Source LLC
Chambersburg PA
CBHW071219130626
46555CB00004B/1769